HOW THE
CHILDREN
STOPPED THE
WARS

JAN WAHL

HOW THE CHILDREN STOPPED THE WARS

Illustrated by Maureen O'Keefe

TRICYCLE PRESS

Berkeley, California

⊕ TRICYCLE PRESS

P.O. Box 7123
Berkeley, California 94707

Book design by Hal Hershey

Library of Congress Cataloging-in-Publication Data

Wahl, Jan.
  How the children stopped the wars / Jan Wahl ; illustrated by
  Maureen O'Keefe
      p.   cm.
  Summary: Inspired by a mysterious stranger, Uillame starts a
  children's crusade to stop the wars that have called away their
  fathers, uncles, and brothers.
      ISBN 1-883672-00-7
      [1. War—Fiction.]   I. O'Keefe, Maureen, ill.   II. Title
  PZ7.W1266Ho   1993
  [Fic]—dc20   93-2479
                                                            CIP
                                                             AC

First published by Farrar, Straus and Giroux, 1969
First Tricycle Press printing, 1993

Manufactured in the Republic of Korea

1 2 3 4 5 — 97 96 95 94 93

To the flower kids

russ and karen

CONTENTS

I	The Stranger	1
II	Between Two Stars	7
III	The Parade Is Growing	15
IV	The Helpful Cloak	23
V	Forest Noises! Attacked!	29
VI	Up, Feet, Up	39
VII	Cold Hot Groggk	49
VIII	The Trip Inside Boats	61
IX	The Stopping	73

PICTURES

Clouds spilled forth that day. . . .
(following page 1)

"That is war," said the stranger. . . .
(following page 9)

All of them were determined to follow Uillame.
(following page 17)

Then a shout—"Look up!"
(following page 23)

The children stuffed their pockets. . . .
(following page 33)

Broad-brimmed hats for everybody. . . .
(following page 43)

The children dropped their bowls of Groggk. . . .
(following page 55)

"'Tis an outbreak of the *Spotted Pox!*"
(following page 69)

They embraced.
(following page 79)

I
THE STRANGER

Clouds spilled forth that day as though poured from a silver pitcher. Some were sea blue, some red pepper scarlet, some lime green. Twisting and puffing into every kind of growing shape.

Twisting into shapes of ships. Shapes of soldiers' shields. Shapes of fir trees.

Shapes of bread loaves. Whizzing omelettes. Amazing flowers. Shapes of rolling, spinning barrels which made loud noises as if gigantic stones were shifting back and forth inside.

In the evening, all clouds faded. Then—a very bright comet appeared, swishing through the rapidly changing

skies. Five sleepy crows flew with a rustle toward this falling star, hoping it was something to eat. The comet vanished, flicking its tail down past hills.

So the surprised crows dropped, folding their wings and immediately snoozing.

On the hillsides, sheep gathered and huddled close, in order to get warm. Fires were lit in distant dwellings.

Outside, it was chilly and the ground was hard as a frosty brick. Those who were lucky were sleeping under straw, as if inside nests. The boy who tended the sheep, however, had wandered off to hunt for the sweet grass they loved and so they were too far from their master's house to return home for the night. Therefore the sheep and the boy had to lie out in the open.

The boy knew if he lay down he would probably wake up with a frostbitten nose.

His name was Uillame (say it like Wee-yam). The sheep were sisters and brothers to him.

He went hurrying back and forth rubbing his hands. He heard an owl calling, in the vague woods below: "Warning yoo! Warning yoo!"

He saw a shadow gliding and sliding along the briar-rimmed road at the foot of the hill: it was not a gray wolf, but a tall man wrapped up in an old brown cloak. Uillame watched, grabbing a stout branch to use as a weapon.

It might be a robber—since plenty of robbers crept through these shadowy woods; and if you happened to have gold in your pockets, it was better to stay away. Uillame kept one eye on his flock, guarding it. He tried not to tremble, and gripped the branch, which was as tall as himself.

Slowly and wearily, the stranger struggled up the steep hill. Yellow and red-ochre and orange glittered along the edges of the sky like heat lightning in summer.

The stranger would attempt three or four steps and then pause, for his legs must have been aching. He would rub his knees and manage to climb a little farther up the hill.

His brown cloak was torn. His feet, which were torn also and bleeding, had no sandals, even, to protect them. He wore a grotesque, long beard; however, what you could make out, above the beard, appeared to be a kind-enough face. So Uillame instead of chasing him away offered him a log to sit down on. The man sat, while several small woolly lambs clustered about him. He did not smell very good or look very appetizing.

"Are you feeling all right?" Uillame boldly asked. The stranger seemed not to hear. Instead, he started to sob,

then the earth quaked, the dry woods below rattled hor-
ribly, and the moon nearly cracked in half, sharing his
pain. A wild, wild wind blew till the stout branch got
yanked roughly out of Uillame's hand.

II

BETWEEN TWO STARS

Uillame had a crumbly, precious chunk of Hindoo cheese which he was to make his breakfast on; however, he gave it at once to this stranger. Without a word the stranger straightaway gobbled it down, then carefully wiped his fingers on the tattered rumpled smelly cloak. You could smell every smell of the world in that cloak—damp caves, and sticky swamps, and sweating camels. Marvelous grape arbors, too. And sweet golden honey. And perfumes from all the beautiful flowers.

The stranger seemed to be stretching his gaze off to some object, to some *thing* thousands of miles away.

"How wretched the state of the world is!" cried the stranger in a voice suggesting immense pain. For his part, Uillame was too ignorant to guess why, since he was too busy, each day, climbing with his flock up glorious, grassy hilltops; or he was dreaming about thick steamy soup which he sometimes tasted with the ladle out in his master's kitchen; or he was concocting different games to play on his day off (Christmas) such as Drop-the-peg-next-find-it-with-your-eyes-shut, and Smack-the-snow-ball-against-the-oak-next-tell-your-fortune-from-it, and Run-where-the-wind-will-blow-you.

"It's sad!" the stranger went on, gazing up into the sky where the moon at that moment was like a bright plate on a dark shelf. "Far from here, a great many men, by this I mean uncles, brothers, cousins, and fathers, are fighting great and monstrous and terrible——"

He paused, because it seemed to hurt him to utter this word—"Bat-tles!" Deliberately he made it sound like *bat tails*. The word choked him. He gasped for air.

The stars in the sky had drifting down from them a yellow powder. The stranger spoke on, the ground below continued to shake. The sheep started whimpering and needed to be comforted.

Then swiftly the stranger lifted his long skinny arm and pointed between two of the largest stars.

Those two, gigantic, turned red as fire, redder than Uillame's own carroty hair.

Dimly at first—then more and more clearly—Uillame saw a peculiar sight between the pair of red stars: as though a tremendous mirror were being held by an invisible hand up in the heavens. He glimpsed the glitter of steel swords and flashing helmets, followed by twists and popping puffs of bomb smoke. And much, much worse! Terrifying, grisly sights!

Uillame covered his eyes behind his sleeve. He remembered at that instant his father, who was serving in the wars. They took him away so long ago that Uillame had forgotten about him—as if he were dead, like his mother.

"That is war," said the stranger, stabbing his forefinger at the scene in the heavens. His cloak began to look, increasingly, like a soldier's cape. Suddenly, Uillame thought the stranger might be a runaway from a distant army.

However, when you examined his bearded face, you were almost comforted; you started to feel warm inside; you wanted to be his friend. The stranger did not look like somebody who was a coward.

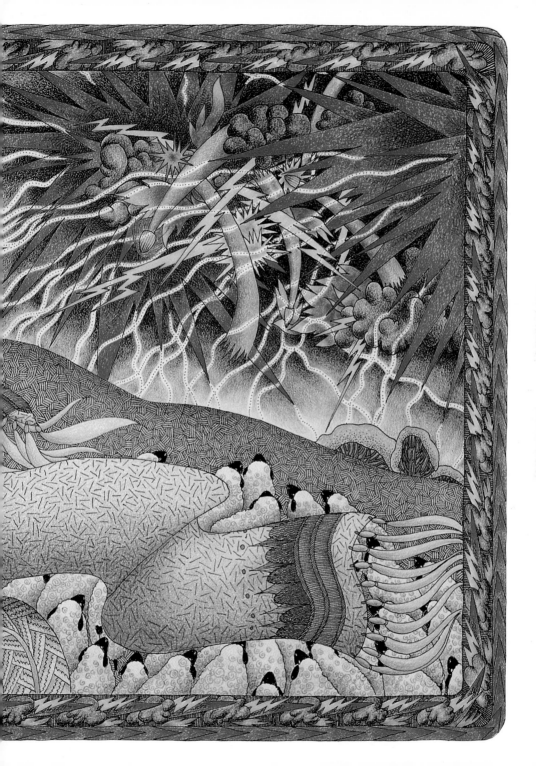

The awful, smoky scene up in the sky lingered on.

It flickered, flared, would not go away.

Thunder growled uncomfortably close: it was just beyond the next hill over, as if it were approaching and soon would be under your feet, and crevices would yawn open and you would topple in and never be seen again! Uillame tried to put his arms around his flock to protect them. They shuddered beneath their wool.

The stranger groaned. "War never—never—never—never seems to have a stopping! First, one side wins. Then, the other side wins. Next, when they are through and have a chance to catch their breath, somebody starts it all over again. It's been going on like this now as long as I can remember!"

The stranger's eyes resembled the two fiery stars themselves.

He paused again, then went on.

"Once, in times that are gone, there was war here—in this very spot!" He glanced briskly around, from one end of the landscape clear to the other, as though haunted by the sight still. Uillame could feel advancing armies ready to clash, moving silently past the underbrush in the woods, preparing to seize the very hill they stood upon.

"Thick trees withered! Grass got scorched black! Houses everywhere were knocked apart! Chimneys crumbled to the ground! Afterward, there was the silence of an open tomb. Lots of people were carried off stacked one on top of the other, like pieces of fallen timber."

The stranger sat down upon the log again, dog-tired after remembering all that he had to recall.

He instantly seemed, in a remarkable manner, to shrink, whoosh, whissh! Till he was no bigger than Uillame himself! Even in this small size, the stranger had the look of a weary but impressive figure.

Above them the mighty struggle continued. Skyrockets appeared, bursting through the space between the red stars; metal loudly clanged; cannons boomed; sky and earth both trembled violently.

"Grown-up people are continually fighting about something," interrupted the stranger. He heaved a sigh full of meaning, and kept dwindling.

"Well then—why doesn't somebody stop it?" asked Uillame, bending down beside the miniature figure.

"*Why don't you?*" screamed the stranger in the tiniest, squeakiest voice imaginable, so that Uillame was scarcely able to hear it above the din.

Then suddenly the stranger was gone. Nothing was left of him except the peculiar-smelling cloak and a few curly stray hairs from his beard.

For a long while Uillame sat pondering what the stranger had told him. *"Why don't you?"* stuck in his ear like a burr; it grew inside his head. The vision of the battle scene had vanished from between the stars. He turned to his flock. They lay in a circle together, asleep.

Then he heard a flapping.

The brown cloak was flying off, before he could grab it.

III

THE PARADE IS GROWING

By the time the sun arose, strong and shiny, Uillame's mind was made up. *"Why don't you?"* the stranger had asked. That was a pretty good question.

Having glimpsed that terrible vision in the sky, Uillame could not remain idle. There was a fluttering in his chest and his head was hot, but what he had to do was clear.

He walked the sheep back down the path to his master's house, sadly. He loved them; it would not be easy to leave them. He put them in the care of Old Bottle-Tom, the gardener, who leaned against his spade and took off his hat and solemnly promised he'd let them graze at the back of the garden.

"I will need a hat," Uillame said to himself.

He persuaded Lupilla, the upstairs chambermaid, to sew him a broadbrimmed one of green felt. He fastened a bluejay's feather onto it for luck.

From shreds of ancient draperies, Lupilla stitched together for him an imposing warm garment of many colors. She also made, under his direction, a banner with two scarlet stars on, like the stars of the vision.

The master was very sorry to let Uillame go, and emerged from his study dripping ink from a broad quill pen. "You are a good sheep-herder, and you ought to stick to that," said the master. "You are a fool or very advanced for your age. I am not sure which. What did they say you want to do?" he asked, shuffling his carpet-slippered feet.

"Stop the wars," spoke up Uillame. Upon that, the master retired grumbling back to his study, leaving an ink trail behind him on the oaken floor.

From an upper casement window, the master's wife waved her orange calico handkerchief. "Good-bye!" she called.

The stableman Florenko gave Uillame a very sturdy and handsome pony, whose name was Paraquin. "They will never miss just one," Florenko whispered. Mounting Paraquin, Uillame quickly rode toward town.

A strange black cloud, gloomy and wild, swept over the little town in advance of Uillame's coming. A deep darkness grew, spreading out beyond the edges of town like a thick fog. Everybody rushed outside to see what was the matter.

Uillame, alone, seemed to be lighted up, because of his rainbow colors, as he jogged along on his pony. Somebody ran alongside and asked about the flag with its two stars; what did that mean?

Uillame happened to be passing the town pump, so he hitched Paraquin to it and leaped onto the platform nearby. He told everybody around about the stranger— about the vision between the red stars.

"Fellow children!" he urged. "I am setting out now for where the wars are," he announced matter-of-factly. "I am wondering who will travel with me? Who will keep Paraquin (this is Paraquin) and me company? Who misses and wants back a father, an uncle, a cousin, a brother? Who has the courage to leave home? Who isn't afraid to

see what it's all about?" He waited a minute and then added: "Are you listening?"

"We are listening!" cried the children.

Uillame then confessed he had no special notion of how to stop the wars. But each child missed somebody away fighting, and many shouted, "I'm not afraid!" Uillame whipped the banner above his head and shook it. His eyes were dazzling bright.

He started moving out of town and hundreds of children piled after. They waved farewell to their tiny baby brothers and sisters and to their mothers and grandmothers. Sons left home with shouts. Mothers wept into their aprons.

Hands reached out to pull the children back, but one adventurer after another slipped into place. They left chores unfinished and lessons unread, and those who were to be punished and had to stand in corners rushed to the front of the line. They threw on caps and kerchiefs and grabbed extra sweaters or shawls and joined Uillame and his small steed, Paraquin.

A lot of dogs came barking along, some dancing on their hind feet. Interested cats slinked along in and out. Banners were improvised out of odds and ends and were hoisted aloft. Uillame rode at the head of it all, while the others walked or rode behind on mules and donkeys. A blind child was led by the hand. A goat or two tried to join in.

Mothers who had already given up their husbands and eldest sons to the fighting stood by with stricken faces, watching, unable to believe their eyes. Yet nothing could bribe the children back . . . no bright objects, no cakes, no pleadings. All of them were determined to follow Uillame. To them he was something special.

The Mayor, Mr. Enderwycke, had wanted to deliver a little speech for the occasion—but the children would not wait any longer. Therefore the Mayor was left atop his rickety stool talking to himself, whirling his arms in the air.

"Good-bye, good-bye!" their families called. Some of the grandmothers boosted themselves up to the tops of the roofs and sat watching the children march off down the road.

They raised a big cloud of dust behind them. "Good-bye!" a faint echo came drifting.

Good-bye

Good-bye

Good-bye

IV

THE HELPFUL CLOAK

n every town and village they passed through, more children were added to the parade. Word rushed, lickety-split, ahead, so that new recruits eagerly awaited their coming. In fields where plump, flush-faced farmers' wives were cutting the hay, children scuttled out from under their mothers' billowing skirts like animals set free.

Some came riding joyfully upon donkeys or goats, or, like Uillame, jogging upon their ponies; but most of them undertook the journey the difficult way—by foot. Croaking frogs, fragile-winged butterflies, brightly feath-

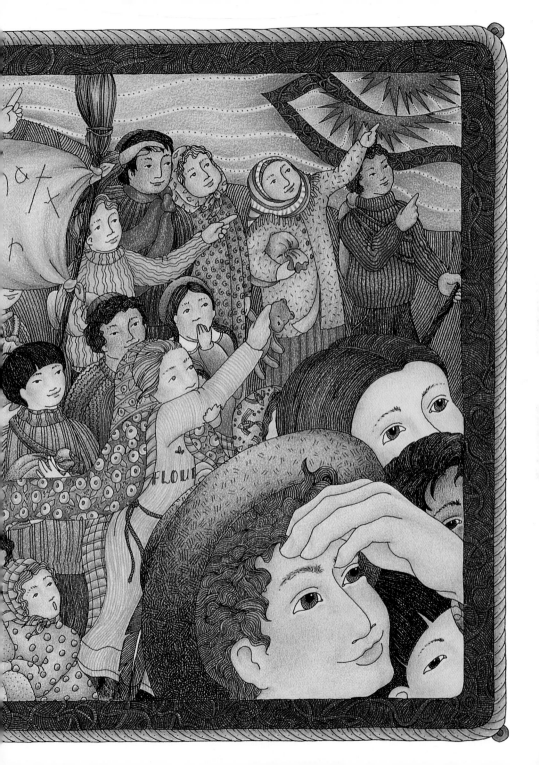

ered birds joined the procession, too, hopping, swooping, spinning.

Some of the marchers brought tall tallow candles for the dark, with boxes of flints. Brilliant-colored flags got flung high. Some brought nets in which to catch fish. Others who like Uillame had been shepherds brought shepherds' crooks to lean on when they grew tired.

Painted clowns and tall-hatted magicians came along to amuse them, hoping to pick up a few pennies, tumbling and conjuring endlessly.

Old men with flowing cottony beards hobbled with them as fast as they could manage; they had become like children again.

The line was stretching longer and longer. The yellow sun blazed every day. Toward early evening, breezes came from over the high mountains to flutter the banners and whip smartly the flag with two red stars. Uillame held on tight to the standard and rode proudly.

Late at night, the tallow candles were ignited with flints; then a long line of torches twinkled across the dim fields marvelously.

Side by side the exhausted children slept, in straw-stacks. Butterflies flew into the old men's beards. Uillame sometimes lay half awake, half in dream, supposing he was huddled with his sheep.

On some days Uillame got lost. "Which way to the war, please?" he might ask a traveler; fortunately, the traveler was usually able to point in the right direction: toward the farthest rim of the horizon.

In twos and threes the children marched abreast. Soon Uillame was unable to remember all their names.

There was Robbin the Small and Robbin the Cheerful and Robbin the Lazybones and Elsa and Mettah and Pip and Frunts and Flogerik and Quirkel and Gwithimagg. There were plenty of Jacks, Marys, and Toms.

They went together singing every kind of wonderful tune. When they became footsore, they rested their feet in cool running brooks. No swimming was allowed, since if all of them jumped in, the water would have flowed over the banks.

One day they plunged into a deep, winding valley. There the road split off in several directions.

Uillame the leader sat on Paraquin, fretting. He could not decide which really was the way to the battleground, or how far it was yet, or what they would do when they got there.

Then a shout—"Look up!"—was carried from one end of the line to the other. Paraquin snorted and looked up also. Across the narrow sky was flying a large brown bird.

However, it was not, upon closer inspection, a bird at all. It was the stranger's cloak, folded into a shape cleverly resembling a bird, slowly flapping its wings of cloth high above their heads.

As soon as the children had spied it, it picked up speed, whizzing onward. Paraquin followed it as rapidly as he could, and the long line traveled forward out of the deep winding valley. The cloak-bird disappeared.

But it had led them to a road which ran like a painted stripe over the bulging and dipping hills.

V

FOREST NOISES! ATTACKED!

The path, often, was rugged and treacherous.

Here and there, in certain countries, they passed strange ruins left by long-ago fighting. A broken marble column would be left standing, maybe with ivy holding it together. Once, they found a roof with no house of any kind below it—a roof of neat orange tiles, laid upon the ground as if dropped there by the hand of a giant.

Everywhere mothers wept when their children marched off, and the mothers' weeping made the sound of a soft rain behind them. Uillame led his followers onward, unyielding, with their gaze fixed on the farthest rim of the horizon.

They marched, by the sides of steep plum-colored mountains, sometimes under waterfalls, where they got drenched. They would try not to slip on the wet stones. This wasn't easy, since they had to carry those who had gotten blisters on their feet.

They trudged into moors, dark and misty, where owls hooted and hinted of gruesome terrors that lay on the other side. They often believed that in the far distance they heard bugles, drum-rolls, and the crash of something like cymbals, yet they were never sure this was what they heard.

They journeyed into each new forest singing.

"Bim, Bam, Bim!" Like that.

"Bim, Bam, Bim!" they'd sing out boldly to keep their courage up. Uillame would sing the loudest, beating time.

"BIM! BAM! BIM!"

They approached the thickly tangled places where there were no road signs, no landmarks of any sort— where only wolves, hyenas, stags, and wild boars with sharp tusks roamed. Black, nodding trees bent over them.

Cuckoos, bobolinks, thrushes, nightingales serenaded near at hand, unseen. Figs, grapes, luscious melons, bush pears, apples abounded. The children stuffed their pockets and they ate till they were drowsy from eating.

They sometimes napped in the mossy dells; but when long shadows lengthened, they would stir themselves and march ahead into the falling red sun.

Soon the next forest would rise in front of them. They walked into clumps of spruce trees and pine trees, into clusters of oaks and thickets of black birches. They had to pick their way carefully through brambles, briars, creeping eglantine, knotted big roots, and evil prickly thorns which tore their hands.

Rocks became surprise ambling tortoises.

Gray soft mounds were hunched-up rabbits.

Anthills erupted and let loose armies of ants which bit them till it hurt.

Sometimes they slept right there in the forest. Moonspots lay where there were spaces left among the leafy branches, but otherwise the prison of trees stretched like a vast engulfing shadow.

Moles, badgers, and other queer animals went snuffing by in the dark, speaking mysterious languages.

Whenever they located a good-sized clearing, Uillame set about arranging a campsite and a fire. Sentries were posted, because of grizzlies and because of the ruthless, sly robbers who hid out in great woods. There was not much for robbers to steal from them, but robbers will steal anything, for they hate departing empty-handed.

The little travelers would go to sleep, wrapped up in blankets and shawls and banners, huddled as close to the fire as they could manage. The birds nestled nearby; the butterflies had already drifted away in the first stiff wind. Above, through the gaps in the tree crowns, jingled pale, icy stars.

More scary than the sudden night sounds—swishings, slidings, howlings, rustlings—were those silences in-between. Then there was a hushed waiting hanging in air. Like just before that moment when the clock strikes the hour. Then—a branch would sway . . . a fallen twig would crack.

In an instant Uillame was up, demanding, "Who is there? Speak out! Speak out!"

One night Uillame lay upon the grass, missing the cozy warmth from the bricks near the hearth in the cook's kitchen in his master's house. He lay half awake, half dreaming, wondering what his plan was. Still he had no plan! But the wars had to be found, the blood-spilling stopped. The important part, he knew, was fixing your mind upon a thing and holding fast to it, no matter what. The first thing he thought he might say to his father was, "Hello, Father, come home."

Uillame knew how to nap and keep his ears open at the same time, because, back home, wolves had prowled the moon-glistening hills hunting for his sheep. It was the silent moments that made him shudder.

There *was* a night pause. Suddenly, some coughing behind the bushes, and a clinking, clanking of coins in pockets; and Uillame realized they were to be set upon by robbers.

The children on the ground slept blissfully.

The band of sentries was at once alerted. One of these was Flora the miller's daughter, whose dress had been fashioned from a flour sack. Her banner, too, was a flour sack tied to a broom handle. She instantly began poking some of the children with it. Uillame woke up others.

The robbers opened their attack by throwing sharp stones and pebbles. The only ammunition the children had at hand was clumps of dirt.

The pebbles and stones stung! The savage pelting kept on. You never knew where you would get hit next! The sentries held bows and arrows, made from saplings—and got ready to shoot them off into the dark.

It was Flora who had an idea.

"If we all snore, at the same time, one big snore, it will sound like a giant is sleeping here in the middle of us. When I raise my banner, let's do it!"

So they did, a great, snorting snore such as man had never before heard. Followed by a big, letting-out whistle.

The great barrage of hard, stinging ammunition suddenly stopped. *This* had completely unsettled the robbers; they didn't even stop to think about it. The robbers fled away in confusion—bumping, whacking, thumping into one another, losing most of their coins.

The next morning Uillame and the children set out to gather up the coins the robbers had spilled. They could use them to buy sausages and other provisions. Picking up the coins left strewn about led the children into a field of red, ripe strawberries growing wild by the edge of the forest.

With some coins, Uillame bought from farmers' wives fresh cows' milk to go with the berries.

Then they sat down and started to have a feast by the side of a ditch, until a gusty wind blew the strawberries out of their bowls. They had to move on, before the storm caught them on this side of the mountains.

VI

UP, FEET, UP

Like the mournful blasts from some horn held by a white demon, the wind blew and blew.

The banners whipped briskly. The travelers had to grip tight, the staffs vibrating in their hands. Mountains loomed: immense, tilted walls towering over them. The narrow path climbed higher, higher, and higher, until it lost itself among rocky crags.

Since most of the children had no proper winter boots on, they had to bind their freezing feet with heavy strips of cloth. Up they headed into bristling thick snows, right into the middle of the frozen glacier which shimmered like glass.

The higher they reached—picking their way inch by inch along tottering brinks, among jagged, cracking ice, among deep, fearsome crevices in which, if you plummeted, you would slide all the way down into the earth, over sharp, splintering ledges—the brighter and clearer the air became.

Then the air stretched thinner and thinner. Therefore they proceeded slowly, snail-like. The icicles played tunes. The snow trail glittered. The round sun sparkled but was itself cold as ice.

From the mountain meadows below echoed the baa-baahing of sheep and the tinkling of the bells around their necks. Farther off, church chimes solemnly tolled.

For an instant Uillame paused and burst into tears. He was picturing his flock in the garden, wandering aimlessly among the hedges. The tears froze upon his cheeks in crystal droplets.

But he urged the children on, up, in, and out of the fierce ravines!

The pony Paraquin grew panicky, terrified of stepping at that extreme height. Uillame tied a kerchief over the poor beast's eyes.

The sheep gave Uillame an inspiration: he sent below, paying by means of the robbers' coins, for a tinkling bell for each of his followers. Now they would not get lost from each other, even during a storm. When the bells were all fixed on, it sounded like a great Christmas sleigh crawling upward.

Down below lay the last tiny villages with bright shiny roofs . . . the final view of the world they knew! The winding rivers, the spread-out patchwork quilts of fields . . . far behind, mothers, sorrowing.

The robins, rooks, sparrows, pigeons, and other birds that had accompanied them turned back, their wings nearly snapping in the blustering winds. The frogs became frozen in ice till spring. The old gentlemen who were in their second childhood tried hobbling back to their log fires and snug beds at home. The magicians knew there was no money to earn, for Uillame was keeper of the little treasury, so they deserted, too. The clowns tumbled with them, doing cartwheels to keep warm and limber. Some of the children ran away with them, to become apprentice clowns and magicians.

Many of the hundreds of children who remained vigorously sneezed and blew their noses. Cautiously they trudged ahead, their bells ringing.

Even the pines and fir trees deserted the mountain. The wind chased the children and tossed snowflakes down their necks.

They climbed straight up into a place of total whiteness. There, their breath formed pictures in the air.

They scarcely had energy to take one step more, when the growling wind mercifully ceased.

It was absolutely quiet and empty then—except for the faint ring of sheepbells. The children were so hungry that they crammed their mouths full of snow and learned, to their sorrow, it was bitter cold, without any taste. The parade rested while some of them sculpted with the snow, making a table with roast goose and roast pig on it, and puddings and breads and pies. They watched their handiwork for a long time, hoping it would never melt.

At length, they managed to struggle just beyond the pass. They jingled and jangled on tiptoe between its steep sides, keeping eyes peeled for possible signs of avalanche. Only tradesfolk and the foolhardy ever dared to enter this realm.

At last on the other side the children found an abbey. They plodded up to the thick oaken door, leaning heavily on sticks and banners. Uillame knocked, and the children all rang their bells. A ruddy friar, with gnarled, kindly hands, creaked the door open and invited them in. The travelers, already turned blue, were given warm food and beds of soft pine needles. After prayers, the good brothers sang songs; Brother Rowland, who had opened the door, sang loudest. The children beat time with their hands and got warmer.

There were so many children crowded inside the abbey that most of the furniture—sturdy plank tables and benches—had to be taken outside to make room. The friars showed eagerness to hear what the children were doing; so Uillame told them about the stranger, about the vision between the two red stars, about missing his own father, about asking the other children to go with him. The friars listened, and whispered among themselves.

"Should we tell about the robbers, too?" asked Flora, the miller's daughter, itching to tell.

"No," said Uillame. "It's not important. This," he told Brother Rowland, "is one of the bravest among us! Once," he added, wistfully, "we found some wild strawberries." Then he fell asleep.

During the night, while the children slumbered, the friars stayed up, stitching for them gowns of gray with two red stars on the front. Broad-brimmed hats for everybody, fashioned out of metal soup bowls; brims were snipped from stiff cardboard.

Since Uillame already had the two-star insignia upon his banner, he didn't need one on his garment. Somebody sewed a ribbon across the front of his, instead, saying— boldly:

LEADER

In the morning, after the oatmeal was eaten, the children strutted proudly back and forth, trying on their new garments. The bells had been attached at the ends of the sleeves.

Even Paraquin got a hat.

The friars, who were famous for it, baked plenty of loaves of fresh, salt-rising bread for them to carry. They were also known for making splendid cheeses, and they packed various mild and tart ones in baskets with the bread.

In the next room, where the baking and cheese-making was done, the walls were as white as the snow outside. There were deep ovens, and stirring vats, and big wooden spoons, and cheesecloth. The golden cheeses were rolled into huge, and smaller, balls; the loaves of bread had hot brown crusts.

Now the children were thawed out and the procession set forth once more. The friars guided them along between the mountain walls. "Bim! Bam! Bim!" the children shouted.

The friars ran back inside to clang the iron abbey bells in loud farewell. White doves fluttered, scurrying out from the noisy belfry.

Jogging down the descending trails was easy—though it was so cold still that the wind seemed to be howling inside the children. Snow blew in great flurries, then it settled down, and they were approaching the warm country on the other side. They could see a big town below.

"Now do you have a plan?" asked Flora.

"Not yet," sighed Uillame.

VII
COLD HOT GROGGK

The children believed that they were approaching the sea because the ditches by the roadside were constantly full, now. On they went, ringing their bells.

Ahead of them, clouds were gathering, scattering, bursting, drawing up more water. The world seemed to be flooded with tears. Wherever the children ventured, they heard about men taken away to serve in the wars. Such men as came wandering back very often returned staggering and limping, with bandages or with wooden legs, or wearing a black patch over the eye that was missing.

"War is a grown-up's job," Uillame was told everywhere. "How can you, a pipsqueak of a boy, attempt to stop this thing that started before you were born?"

People jeered and snickered at them, and refused them food, and threw stones, or tried to get them to work for small wages in the cities. Uillame tried patiently explaining, wherever he could collect an audience, that some day those same boys and girls with him would grow up and then the war would be *theirs*.

"But fighting is an ancient custom! It started ages back—about the time the world began!" somebody would shout. Well, Uillame would answer, it's hardly worth handing down just because it is an old custom! Wasn't it more important to walk up a green hill and be free to watch your sheep? Uillame would raise his banner straight and high in the air and lead his followers into the country again. Nightingales, from the meadows, poured out their "Joog, Joog, Joog."

Toward dusk one evening, in the middle of an alfalfa field which they had to cross to get someplace, the procession of children met a little girl who was busily clapping her hands. She was searching the sky.

Uillame thought maybe she had glimpsed the flying brown cloak. "Did you happen to see something like a big brown bird?"

"Why no. I'm clapping for stars to come out," the little girl replied.

And so they did. *It* did: the first star of the evening burst out shining.

"Well, have you happened to see, lately, two red stars?" Uillame them asked. "With some pictures forming between?"

"No, not really," said the little girl. Her name was Morosina. She studied with great interest the dusty, ragged band of marchers following.

Uillame explained, as he patiently but urgently always did, where they were heading. And why. Morosina agreed she missed *her* father, terribly; but she worried who would gather the eggs from the hen coops if she did not. She studied the stars and went away and brought each child one fresh egg.

"From now on, gather your own eggs," she informed the chickens. "I've more important things to do!"

And stepped into line, marching beside Flora the miller's daughter.

The farther south they reached, the queerer were the names of places they marched through, till not even Morosina knew how to pronounce the difficult names.

Soon the children approached a city where giant moths whizzed in and out in great numbers. Everything there seemed ready to crumble away. Every kind of dwelling had once been built there: alabaster—mud—cedar—odd-shaped blocks—bricks—and shingle.

There were copper doors and leather doors and wood doors and iron doors and straw doors, falling off at the hinges. Some buildings had no doors at all, just gaping holes in front.

Nobody was walking in the streets. Yet Uillame and his followers entered the city feeling that, behind every window, people were watching.

In this city, called Faltzmodder, the able-bodied men and beggar boys had been forced to join the army. Workers were needed desperately to learn all the trades and take their places. There was no one left to sweep the streets, to mend the leather harnesses, to shoe the horses, to fix the leaking roofs.

When the children had passed through the rubble in the streets as far as the Town Hall Square, the ladies of Faltzmodder rushed outside.

Each one grabbed the nearest child or two and pulled them into her house, offering juicy roast beef with turnips and sweet potatoes for supper and cozy beds with eiderdown quilts for sleeping in. The children were too tired to resist. Their clothes needed mending; it would be nice not to sleep in a deep ditch that night!

First, the Faltzmodder ladies soaked the children in wooden tubs and tidied them up, picking the cinders and burrs from their hair. In the house where Uillame was taken the bed was hard, but he woke up having slept a good night's sleep.

That morning, when the sun took its place in the sky like a yellow cork bobbing there, the Faltzmodders were out bustling in the kitchens with aprons on, stirring something in kettles. They were fixing Hot Groggk. This brew was the specialty of Faltzmodder.

It was a steamy, scented, sharp, sugary, spicy brew. Just a whiff of it and your nose would not stay away.

You wanted to taste it upon your tongue, you wanted to have it warm your insides and make them glow. It had cloves in it, lots of brown honey and ginger, the juice squeezed from plums, molasses, chocolate, bacon rinds, apple peelings, nutmeg, butter, cardamom, and something from an unlabeled crockery jar. It was so thick you had to eat it with a spoon.

Each child in each house was given this to drink. The Groggk made things look blurry and made each wish to sleep again; but the ladies remarked that this was nothing to worry about! The ladies drew the children to them, putting the smaller ones on their laps, looking sad, mist covering their eyes. They chattered away, letting the children know how miserable it was with their menfolk away, how comforting it was to have all those children there. Furthermore, they promised delicious Hot Groggk *every morning* if the children would stay! The children were growing dizzier and dizzier.

They remembered as if in a dream the houses they once had lived in. Some of their houses had hemlocks and magnolias and spruce trees growing in the yards. Some of the houses still smelled of thick pipe tobacco smoked by their fathers. Some of the houses had goldfish swimming around in bowls. Some of the houses had grandfathers who told funny stories. Outside on chilly days the wind would bang against the houses and send things rolling across the yards, but inside it would be cozy and just perfect and warm like Hot Groggk . . . like lovely Hot Groggk! The children were growing more and more homesick.

"Every day, you will get Hot Groggk. In return, there are a few chores to attend to," the ladies whispered.

"You won't ever have to worry about being bored or *idle*," the ladies promised. The mistiness in their eyes shifted to a shrewd glitter as they described (pouring more Groggk) what fun it would be to stay in Faltzmodder. The boys could be grown-up butchers, bakers, ironmongers, shoemakers, carpenters, blacksmiths, and potters. The girls could try their hand at being dyers, seamstresses, weavers, soap-makers, housekeepers, and cooks. The littlest of the children could carry in the wood after it had been chopped, and all could chase away the sparrows and the crows.

The giant moths fluttered over the breakfast tables. The children, in the middle of drinking their Groggk, saw some wooden hoops and rag dolls in the corners of the

kitchens. "Where are your *own* children?" they suddenly asked.

"Oh, the poor dears!" replied the ladies. "They had to be taken away to the hospitals. They were working too hard and needed a rest. They never drank enough of this delicious Hot Groggk! It peps you up! It makes you want to work and help out; after all, we can't do every bit of the work ourselves."

Uillame, in the house where he stayed, pushed his bowl of Groggk aside. "But we have our own work!" he shouted. He left his Faltzmodder lady, who chased him part-way to the Town Hall Square, where he had tethered Paraquin to a post. Uillame quickly sounded the alarum upon his trumpet.

The children dropped their bowls of Groggk with a terrific clatter. They came tumbling out of the houses to join him before it was too late. What a racket there was— what a sniveling from the ladies!

"You are welcome to stay! Oh, stay with us!" the ladies shrieked from their doorways. *"We love you!"* Their ready tears welled up once more and flowed and gushed out. The parade rushed away from the city in desperation.

The Faltzmodder ladies leaped from the doorways, shaking their wooden spoons in the air.

As for the Hot Groggk—that delectable, peculiar brew that makes you a fiend for work if you drink too much—it was left standing until it grew quite cold. Not even the ladies of Faltzmodder wanted to drink it.

VIII

THE TRIP
INSIDE BOATS

"Bim! Bam! Bim!" went the children, after their escape.

They shouted it all the way to the edge of the land. Their path led straight to a wide, wide beach; the next leg of the journey would have to be by water. How the sea billowed—surged—rolled—and foamed!

The marching children stood with Uillame upon the dazzling hot sand. They did not pick up the seashells, the starfish, or the dried seahorses that lay about in numbers near their feet. They were waiting with mounting impatience. On the other side, beyond their gaze, some-where, lay the wars.

"Bim! Bam! Bim!" they sang in unison, wishing the water would suddenly divide or make a tunnel for them. They stood there hoping for it. Somehow, they would have to cross the moving sea.

Now and then fishing smacks out there, curious about the gathering of children, came floating nearer, bobbing up and down in the waves. The fishing smacks looked, then retreated again with jerky movements. Gulls hovered, sometimes gliding down and dropping bits of seaweed from their beaks. If only they might travel upon the gulls' backs!

To entertain everybody Morosina sang some of the country songs she had learned by heart; however, they were not very cheerful songs and Flora asked her please not to sing any more. The last of the old moon now hung in tatters. The children remained on the beach all that night and for many nights after. The moon began growing full again and with it their courage returned.

Early one morning, four queer-looking large sailing ships appeared, advancing toward the shore.

Uillame energetically waved the banner bearing the two scarlet stars. Four captains were rowed out in four little boats. They wore splendid velvet jackets with furry collars, and each captain had a monkey sitting on his shoulder, eating an orange. Their ships were loaded to the brim with pomegranates and oranges and limes and peaches and figs and mangoes and almirzam.

Uillame stepped forward to greet the captains. He told them his story from the beginning—about meeting the stranger who wore the brown cloak which flew, and about the two reddish stars in the sky and the stirring vision between them, and he told how his parade had gathered, in town after town, behind him. He told it as briefly as he could.

The four captains and the four monkeys glanced over the throng of children. "You mean to tell us," one captain whistled, "*you* will stop the wars?" They all removed their caps in order to scratch their heads; one of them was bald and had tattooed on his head a bluebird in a nest.

Another captain said, "Listen, do we have this straight? You're just ordinary children? You aren't carrying any weapons or things like that along? No swords? No pistols?"

Uillame replied, "We have just what you see plus a little gold money. We brought only ourselves. We made some bows and arrows to use in the forests, but we've thrown them away. We would like to cross the sea in front of us here . . . then we should be where we want to be! Once we are there, we will know better what to do." His lieutenants, Flora and Morosina, stood beside him, looking alert and faithful.

"Well—what do you think!" one of the captains chortled. "They only brought themselves, the little hearties, and they suppose they will stop the wars!" The sea captains then went into conference for a few minutes. At last they turned around. They grinned.

"We're with you, mates!" said the captains. The children whooped with glee. "Climb aboard, mateys!" instructed the captains cheerfully. "These little boats will take you out to the ships."

"How much will all this cost?" worried Uillame before he allowed the children to be loaded into the little boats. "We only have a few gold coins."

"Won't cost you a penny," answered the captain with the bluebird tattooed on his head. "Everybody help yourselves to the Spanish oranges—once you are aboard. We have to go across the sea anyway and we'll deliver you!"

Uillame was relieved at this good fortune.

The children were counted off, by fours, and finally set aboard the four ships after many trips in the little boats. Then the animals were brought aboard. The sailors, gathered in groups on the decks, hollered and winked at one another. There was a great deal of festivity among them.

The four vessels dipped a trifle in the sea, under the added load. "Are you sure it's all right to carry us?" Uillame asked his captain. In answer, bushels and crates of cargo were brought up on deck and thrown overboard—figs, pomegranates, and other fruit—with much laughter.

The sailors shinnied up the high masts and the coarse patched sails were unfurled. The tillers were manned; the anchors were hauled in, the chains creaking and clanking, and all four ships were steered into the middle of the open sea, riding as smooth as they could over the rippling waves. The children stood and smelled the clean salty air.

When they were several miles out, a squall washed violently over the decks. On Uillame's boat, the monkey

jumped down from the captain's shoulder and ran gib-
bering up to the crow's-nest and peered out.

The ships kept their course toward the setting blood-
red sun. All the sea around turned shades of rose and pink
with rivulets of purple. Then the water grew quiet and
soon they rode as if sliding upon polished glass.

The following day, the sun was bright. The ships
passed some islands, shimmering with poppies and sun-
flowers, where hippos and wild boars waded together off-
shore. Glittering insects, larger than dragonflies, buzzed
and swarmed over the warm decks. The sailors who were
off-duty sat out there, playing whist and euchre, or telling
the children wild sea stories, of sea serpents and the like.

Suddenly, that evening, thick blinding blue fog coiled
around the ships and a great storm lashed the waters,
coming out of nowhere with considerable force. The four
ships rocked and swayed in the gale. Almost everybody
got seasick—even the most toughened among the crews.
Topsails slapped against spirited winds. There was a
monstrous howling and sea spilled sharply into the air;
ships got mixed with wild black swirling water.

The frightened children lay flattened upon their
bunks or upon the floorboards. They clutched at any-

thing fastened down: hooks, posts, stairsteps, beams, knobs, tied ropes, and kegs.

Through the height of the storm Uillame made the rounds of his ship, from prow to stern, without showing fear. He went up to where Paraquin was hitched and again put the kerchief over the pony's eyes. By his quiet manner he helped calm many of the children.

Every wave brought more water sloshing and smashing. Wood split in two. Wind roared. Anyone on deck unlucky enough not to have something to hang onto was flung brutally overboard. The four boats struggled not to lose sight of each other's lanterns; but at the same time they had to be careful not to careen into each other and sink beneath the troubled sea.

Uillame crawled through a passageway and was flung against the door to his captain's quarters. Above the door was painted this motto:

IT IS MONEY MAKES OUR SPEED

The motto was puzzling. One of the children, a boy named Zepho, was crouched nearby. He pulled at Uillame's long sleeve, motioning for him to follow. Zepho said just loud enough to be heard through the storm: "Come and listen."

Uillame followed him. Dripping wet, they hid among the shadows outside a cabin where two of the mates were speaking together.

"You think we can get two thalers apiece for them?" one mate growled. "Or might we get more if we let them grow up first?" The other mate howled with laughter, so hard that even the wind was blotted out.

Now it was clear to Uillame why the four captains had been so eager to take them aboard; why the sailors had hollered and grinned. These were slave ships, taking the children to a far port to be sold as slaves!

"Follow me," Uillame called to Zepho through the gale, and he led him down into the ship's hold. There, the children who were hiding out from the worst of the storm were dazedly watching the remaining cargo of bruised fruit tumble and splatter.

"I have an idea!" To show them, Uillame scooped up some slimy brown-red goo. With this pulpy stuff he daubed hideous spots on his face. When the children heard why he was doing this, they set to work imitating their leader, crushing more berries and fruit and daubing horrible-looking marks on their faces. Uillame went over and put bright-colored spots on Paraquin also. The storm was ebbing away now, having worn itself out; the ships were rocking less and less.

In the morning, when the big waves had quit hurtling themselves over the decks and it was safe to walk about, the children crowded onto the upper deck of Uillame's ship, wearing their spots. They shook the bells sewn on their sleeves.

"Aiy! Aiy! I recognize that!" screamed a terrified sailor. "'Tis an outbreak of the *Spotted Pox!*" And he rushed to warn his fellow sailors. The ship's pilot himself stood trembling at the tiller.

Quickly, by means of mirrors, it was signaled to the other three ships:

C-H-I-L-D-R-E-N H-E-R-E H-A-V-I-N-G
S-P-O-T-T-E-D P-O-X

Next the signal was given to head toward the nearest bay rather than the scheduled slave port—which still lay many furlongs distant. The other ships obliged at once, reckoning their children would soon break out with the Spotted Pox. All day Uillame and the children in his company itched and scratched their spots with real vigor and moaned truly convincingly.

"Hoo! Hoo! Hoo! Hoo!" Till even the sailors themselves started to itch. "Hoo!" moaned the children. "Aiy!" cried the sailors.

All four ships bumped into a bay and deposited the children, who were shooed down the gangways with the donkeys and ponies and mules. Only the four monkeys, in the lavender-colored dusk, bothered to wave any farewell.

The ships departed; Uillame sent his scouts and lieutenants exploring in several directions. Flora scurried back breathlessly to report there was a warm, dry, protected place among big rocks a half mile in from the coast. By now the slave ships' lanterns had ebbed away. Only then did Uillame explain to the rest of the children what had been going on.

Then they all slept soundly, among the rocks, except for Uillame, who could not sleep since he still did not have a plan. It was just before sunrise that he alone heard, shaking the ground, the early merciless boom, the boom-boom-booming of cannons.

"Get up," he told the children. "We are here."

IX
THE STOPPING

illame waited for the twin red stars to show themselves. Or for the stranger's brown cloak to appear. None of these came in the sky, though the morning light exploded and shadows were streaked with wildness. What seemed to be flares glided and fell like sparks pulled into the fire. At last the children were near to the thing itself.

They left the rocks and the cave and reached a long dry empty treeless plain and got very hungry, but after a while they did not think about their hunger or their thirst any more, because they had already been hungry and thirsty many times.

As if a tide were rolling across the plain, the children advanced. Their sheepbells seemed to draw down the buzzards out of the sky; the birds wheeled by with greedy interest. They came to the ruins of a smoking city. Some of the buildings were still in flames. Among the ruins skinny, hollow-eyed children wandered, carefully searching in the rubble, drifting through the gray and yellow streets. These zombie children did not speak; however, they looked up and made little motions toward their mouths with their fingers.

"They are hungry too," whispered Uillame to Flora. The zombie children looked more like ancient men and women with all their bones showing. They did not run away, because there was nowhere to go. These were the children of the people on the other side. Their fathers were at the war and their mothers were wearily sweeping up the rubble, and looking at Uillame and his followers with grave faces.

"Come with us," motioned Uillame. The zombie children stood bewildered. The marching children took them one by one by the hand and they led them, slowly, away from the city. When the zombie children realized what direction they were heading in, they trembled and dragged their feet and shook their heads.

But Uillame's confidence was catching, so they couldn't help following. Uillame rode up and down the line to keep everybody together.

On the plain there were two more villages, burned nearly to the ground. In each, more of the children were seized by the hand. Then the procession approached what had once been a muddy swamp, now dried by the scorched air, and crossed over its cracked crust. Beyond it sat a great rock, and Uillame climbed up to its jagged top and raised his arms and shouted, "Don't hang back! Don't hang back! Soon we'll be face to face with it! It's just a bit farther!" All the children were clinging to each other. Ahead of them they spied the flashing smoke and the bursting of rockets. The trembling of the earth grew worse and worse. Uillame leaped off the rock and got back on Paraquin. "Go now," he yelled into his ear.

The long line of children walked near, nearer to the smoking battleground. Still no exact plan had come to Uillame, no matter how hard he thought.

"Bim!" and "Bam!" and "Bim!" sang out the chorus of children bravely.

"BOOM!" answered the war.

The pony Paraquin jogged along at a sturdy pace. Loyal friend! Recklessly and fearlessly the children followed Uillame and moved on—advancing.

It was now full daylight but *there*—the two red, red stars were shining. Like two immense iron pots in flame, of great weight, about to spill over. They hung at either side of the battleground, which was wider than the plain.

All the land around was parched and cracked. What a gigantic *Booom!* What roars—and bangings—and thunderings! What crashes! And pourings of smoke . . . it was while drifting through the smoke that the children came upon the first crumpled bodies of soldiers.

They discovered tents knocked to the ground. Tipped-over carts and wagons. Unfinished trenches with the shovels for digging broken in two. Mere shreds of things—saddles and campstools and ropes and visors. They heard the cries of living soldiers.

Incredible things flew whizzingly, roughly, around. Orange and yellow rockets burst and the soldiers were busy fighting. Uillame called out: "Perhaps we will not be hurt!"

Flora tugged at his sleeve. She suggested they crouch down on all fours or crawl on their stomachs. No, insisted Uillame. They had to march straight into the thick of it. That was the only way to let their fathers know they were there!

Paraquin was quite small next to the armored war horses kicking up the turf; however, he proceeded with majesty. The little bells could no longer be heard over the tumult. The children huddled close together, each one holding on to the one ahead. They sucked in their breath. The long line of them did not break or hesitate or stumble more than it had to.

Arrows *whiffffed* through the air. Large vans labeled "Explosives" rumbled by. Iron barrels were rolled along. Spikes clanged and clanged together. Uillame's broad-brimmed hat got shot away.

The wounded soldiers who could be mended were carried off on sooty stretchers. The armies attacked, suffered, and bled. There they were—fighting for what, they had forgotten; yet they would not give up that fighting.

Morosina and Flora, dim figures in the whirling smoke, played on their flute and tambourine to keep the ranks together. Then a wind blew some of the battle smoke away. Some of the children had fallen too. The others shuddered more than they had shuddered on the cold mountaintops. Still they kept on, in fairly orderly fashion, lined up behind Uillame, marching through the hurtling ammunition. They raised their elbows to ward off stinging arrows.

"What, in the name of Minerva, can *this* be?" bellowed one general.

Spears, spikes, and arrows continued to be set off, but were shot in scattered volleys, because the soldiers were greatly puzzled by whatever it was that was advancing.

"What manner of army is upon us? Hobgoblins? Dwarfs? Insect recruits to crawl between our legs?"

Uillame listened to them. The children stood there with torn-up flags and banners. Paraquin pawed the ground. The dismal, shadowy, tall shapes—slowly, gradually, became shapes of men, withered from lengthy fighting, gripping their spears and crossbows out of habit. Uillame and the children turned, rubbing grime off their faces, meeting the men's astonished gaze from every quarter. The battleground grew quiet. The dazed, confused soldiers continued to stare at the children. Uillame was clinging to his frayed banner with the two stars on, the two stars which now were overhead, hanging over that battleground, casting a red glow down.

During the lull, Uillame cleared his parched throat. He raised himself up and stood on Paraquin's back, with two children steadying his feet, two others steadying Paraquin. He felt this might be the time to speak. "Sirs!" he said. "We have arrived from very far away, to see for ourselves what it is you are doing here. Back at your homes, land is growing dry, the orchards have gone, your houses are falling to ruin or are burnt. We want to see the victory you are achieving here. Don't you remember us? Don't you remember who we are?" That was about all he could think of to say, after countless nights of lying awake, wondering what his magnificent plan would be. That was *all* he could say to stop them; simply to show them they were there.

Could the fathers fight again, now, with their children watching?

The soldiers on both sides were infinitely tired, and they had begun to feel that the wars might last forever—that they would never get finished. Some soldiers blew their noses; they started wiping some of their grime off,

also. Their eyes were tired and their minds were tired. Now what would happen?

Suddenly one of them shouted, "That's my son! I think! He's bigger now. Well, I *think* that's him. Boy, might your name be Hullbo?"

It was Hullbo, and he ran into his father's arms. He had not seen his father in four years.

One by one, the fathers, the uncles, the older brothers, the cousins were recognized. The furious combat was forgotten.

Which side had been fighting which was forgotten and each man tried to find the child who was related to him. A breeze arose and the banners drifted in it. It took time to match up the living children with their living kinsfolk. When each soldier located the child he was looking for, he would toss his helmet and weapons down with a clatter.

The men stepped up, joyfully, to hug the children they had long missed. Uillame found his own father, who looked old and gray; but that didn't matter.

"Hello, Father," Uillame said.

"Hello, Son," said his father, his eyes glistening with tears. They embraced.

Till evening, the fathers and the children talked. All the fathers asked questions about home and the children tried to answer them and everybody was speaking at the same time.

That night they slept together—huddled like grown bears and bear cubs, the fathers, the sons, and the daughters, among the ruins of that broken battleground.

By morning the fathers were ashamed to remain at this place any longer. They couldn't fight, with their children looking on. Some of the children gathered field flowers from beyond the battleground, which they strewed over the corpses. They all, fathers, uncles, sisters, brothers, cousins, everybody, walked across the wide plain to the sea. Those who belonged on the other side of the sea mounted the ships which had brought the men to war. The others stayed on shore and watched them go. Winds came from the south, filling the sails, pushing them homeward. And—where the war scars were worst, sand blew, filling full the holes in the ground. The cannons sat there rusting. The buzzards and vultures gave up and flew off, disappointed. The two red stars faded.

Listen!

Out over the sea, can't you hear the children and their fathers singing?

You will find peace in many more languages
than can be shown in the illustration following page seventy-nine.
Clockwise from top left:

Japanese

French

Gaelic

Zulu

Russian

Vietnamese

Hebrew

Hawaiian

Norwegian

Spanish

Chinese

English

Indonesian

Onondaga

Welsh

Telugu

Polish

Arabic

Laotian

Arabic

Lenni Lanape

Molbog

Armenian

Hungarian

Czechoslovakian

Italian

German